# Pat, the dog

*For Jane, the niece and Nic, the nephew*

MYRIAD BOOKS LIMITED
35 Bishopsthorpe Road, London SE26 4PA

First published in 1994 by
ANDERSEN PRESS LTD
20 Vauxhall Bridge Road,
London SW1V 2SA

Published in Australia by Random House Australia Pty.,
20 Alfred Street, Milsons Point, Sydney, NSW 2061

ISBN 1 905606 01 X

Printed in China

# Pat, the dog

## GUS CLARKE

MYRIAD BOOKS LIMITED

"Where are you going, Pat?" asked the cat.
"Shopping," said Pat.
"What are you going to buy, Pat?"

"Dog biscuits," said Pat.

"While you're there, Pat," said the cat, "would you mind getting me a nice piece of fish?"

"Not at all," said Pat.

"Where are you going, Pat?" asked the squirrel.
"Shopping," said Pat.
"What are you going to buy, Pat?"

"Dog biscuits and a nice piece of fish," said Pat.

"Pat, old chap," said the squirrel, "be a good fellow and pop in a packet of peanuts for me, would you?"

"OK," said Pat.

"Where are you going, Pat?" asked the duck.
"Shopping," said Pat.
"What are you going to buy, Pat?"

"Dog biscuits, a nice piece of fish and a packet of peanuts," said Pat.

"Do me a favour, Pat," said the duck. "Bring me back a loaf of bread, if it's no trouble."

"No trouble," said Pat.

"Where are you going, Pat?" asked the hen.
"Shopping," said Pat.
"What are you going to buy, Pat?"

"Dog biscuits, a nice piece of fish, a packet of peanuts and a loaf of bread," said Pat.

"Be an angel, Pat," said the hen, "and get me half a dozen eggs, would you dear? There's a love."

"Of course," said Pat.

"Where are you going, Pat?" asked the pig.
"Shopping," said Pat.
"What are you going to buy, Pat?"

"Dog biscuits, a nice piece of fish, a packet of peanuts, a loaf of bread and half a dozen eggs," said Pat.

"Save me a trip, Pat," said the pig. "I'm halfway through the wash and I'm right out of powder. Could you get me a box? Best make it a large one."

"I'll see what I can do," said Pat.

"Where are you going, Pat?" asked the goat.
"Shopping," said Pat.
"What are you going to buy, Pat?"

"Dog biscuits, a nice piece of fish, a packet of peanuts, a loaf of bread, half a dozen eggs and a box of washing powder, large," said Pat.

"I'd go myself, Pat," said the goat, "but I don't like to leave the kids. Could you get me something for their tea? They'll eat anything."

"Leave it to me," said Pat.

"Phew!" said Pat, "I'll be glad to get home."

"Thanks, Pat," said the goat. "I'm very grateful."

"You're welcome," said Pat.

"Well done, Pat," said the pig. "You've saved my bacon."

"Ho ho," said Pat.

"Thank you, Pat," said the hen. "You're a treasure."

"Don't mention it," said Pat.

"Good old Pat," said the duck. "What would we do without you?"

"It was nothing," said Pat.

"Pat," said the squirrel. "You're a perfect poppet."

"Don't be silly," said Pat.

"Thanks, Pat," said the cat. "You're very kind."

"Not at all," said Pat. "I was going anyway."

"Oh no!" said Pat.

"Where are you going, Pat?" asked the cat.
"Shopping," said Pat.

"What are you going to buy, Pat?"

"Dog biscuits," said Pat.